# Lottie
## the Littlest Reindeer

Brimax Books · Newmarket · England

Far, far away in a northern
land covered in ice and snow,
there lived a little reindeer
called Lottie.
Lottie was much smaller than the
other reindeer and this made her
feel very shy.
"I wish I wasn't so small,"
sighed Lottie. "Then I could play
with the other reindeer."

But Lottie had another wish,
something that she wanted more
than anything else in the world.
"I wish . . . I wish I could help
pull Santa's sleigh," said Lottie.
"Maybe you will, one day,"
said her mother.
"But it is Christmas soon and
I'm so little," sighed Lottie.
"Then you must wait until you have
grown up, first," replied her mother.

The other reindeer were much
bigger than Lottie. They were
very excited at the thought of
helping Santa.
"I wonder who will be chosen to
help pull Santa's sleigh this year?"
asked one. "I think it should be
the strongest."
"No, it should be the fastest,"
called another.
"We will hold a contest,"
said a wise, old reindeer.
"That's the best way to choose
who should pull the sleigh."

Lottie had been listening to the other reindeer. This was her chance to help pull Santa's sleigh!

"May I enter the contest, too?" she asked, shyly.

"If you want to," said one reindeer. "But you'll never win. You're far too small!"

The first event was a running race. Lottie stood with the other reindeer on the starting line.
"The first two reindeer to run to that tree and back will be the winners," said the judge.
"On your marks, get set, go!" Lottie ran as fast as she could but she couldn't keep up with the others. Her legs were far too short and she watched sadly as the other reindeer ran past her.

"Perhaps I'll be better at the next event," said Lottie and she watched as a rope was tied between two trees. One by one the reindeer jumped over it. When it was Lottie's turn she took a long run and jumped. Poor Lottie! Her little legs caught on the rope and she landed on the ground with a big bump!
"Bad luck, Lottie!" called the judge. "You're just too little!"

"The test of strength is my last chance," said Lottie. "If only I can win."

"This is Santa's sleigh," said the judge. "All you have to do is pull it as far as you can." Little Lottie was tied to the sleigh. But no matter how hard she tried, she could not move it. She was so unhappy.

"Never mind," said Lottie's mother. "You can always try again next year."

The next day, the winners were called out. Lottie watched sadly as the six fittest and strongest reindeer walked proudly over to the sleigh.
It was full to the top with presents of all shapes and sizes.
"I wish I could go, too," sighed Lottie. "It must be so exciting to help Santa deliver all the presents."

Suddenly a great cheer went up.
"Here comes Santa!" cried Lottie.
"Greetings, my friends!"
cried Santa Claus as he strode
towards them. "It's good to see
you all again!"
He quickly checked the sleigh
then tied the reindeer to it.
"We really must be going,"
said Santa smiling. "We have
a long night ahead of us!"

Lottie looked sadly at the sleigh before it set off. Then just as she was turning to go home, she saw the leading reindeer slip and fall into a snowdrift.

"Oh, no!" cried Santa.

"Now what are we going to do? There are so many presents to deliver and not enough reindeer to pull the sleigh!"

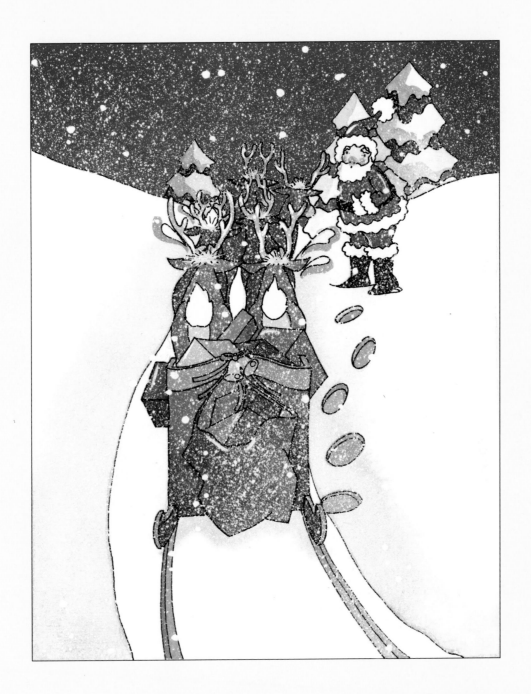

Then Santa saw a little reindeer
standing in the distance.
"Lottie!" he cried. "You are just
what we need! Will you help to pull
my sleigh?"
Lottie could hardly believe her ears.
Her special Christmas wish was
about to come true!
"Oh, yes!" she cried and the
other reindeer smiled as Lottie
was placed at the front of
Santa's sleigh. They all knew how
much Lottie wanted to help.

Lottie stood proudly at the front, her eyes shining happily.

"At last," said Santa. "Now we can deliver all the presents." He sprinkled the reindeer with magic dust and Lottie suddenly felt lighter.

"I can fly!" she cried.

Lottie's mother watched proudly as the sleigh climbed into the air with Lottie leading the way.

What a night Lottie had!
The reindeer stopped at every
house and Santa dropped down
the chimney with his sack
of presents. At last the
reindeer arrived home
as it was getting light.
"Thank you, all!" cried Santa.
"Now everyone can wake up
to a happy Christmas!"
Then Santa smiled and said,
"And a special thank you to
Lottie, the littlest reindeer!"
Lottie had never been so happy!

# Say these words again

| | |
|---|---|
| shy | deliver |
| Christmas | judge |
| smile | jump |
| proudly | dark |
| contest | night |
| front | glow |
| race | red |